As he turned his head, Richard took him by the collar. (**Page** 5)

The Phoenix Library

Robert Louis Stevenson

Dr. Jekyll and Mr. Hyde

retold by John Kennett

Blackie : Glasgow and London

Other titles in this series:

Jane Eyre
Charlotte Brontë

Oliver Twist
Charles Dickens

The Count of Monte Cristo
Alexandre Dumas

The Three Musketeers
Alexandre Dumas

Journey to the Centre of the Earth
Jules Verne

Twenty Thousand Leagues Under the Sea
Jules Verne

Ben-Hur
Lew Wallace

Copyright © 1962 John Kennett
Illustrations copyright © 1973 Blackie and Son Limited
This edition first published 1973

ISBN 0 216 89688 6

Blackie and Son Limited
Bishopbriggs, Glasgow G64 2NZ
Fitzhardinge Street, London W1H 0DL

Printed in Great Britain by Robert MacLehose & Co. Ltd., Glasgow

ROBERT LOUIS STEVENSON, novelist, essayist, and poet, was born in Edinburgh in 1850. Although he never enjoyed good health, he travelled widely, finally making his home in the tropical island of Samoa, where he died in 1894.

His poems for children are collected in *A Child's Garden of Verses*. He wrote many tales of adventure including *Treasure Island*, *Kidnapped*, and *The Black Arrow*.

CONTENTS

CHAPTER		PAGE
1	*Night in the City*	1
2	*The Signature*	9
3	*Blackmail House*	16
4	*Search for Mr. Hyde*	21
5	*Dr. Jekyll*	30
6	*The Carew Murder Case*	37
7	*The Letter*	44
8	*The Terror of Doctor Lanyon*	52
9	*The Face at the Window*	59
10	*The Last Night*	62
11	*The Disappearance*	73
12	*Dr. Lanyon's Statement*	77
13	*Henry Jekyll's Full Statement of the Case*	84

CHAPTER ONE

Night in the City

IT was Mr. Richard Enfield who had the first meeting of any real note—or of which we have any accurate record—with the evil and mysterious being who went by the name of Edward Hyde. It was an experience that left Mr. Enfield—who was a large and active young man, with more than his share of courage—sadly shocked and shaken; more disturbed, in fact, than ever before in the twenty-odd years of his gay and carefree life.

This was the way of it.

Richard had dined in town that night, and then gone on to dance at the Prescott house in Hampstead. By two o'clock in the morning, he had tired of the affair and elected to walk back to his own rooms in the city. He was glad of the chance to walk. The air, he thought, would clear his head, and he was badly in need of the exercise.

He set off gaily enough, swinging his stick and humming the tune of the moment. As time passed, however, his mood changed. It was a cold, black winter's morning and every-where was as quiet as the grave. He began to feel the need for company, for the sound of a human voice.

His way lay through a part of town where there was nothing to be seen but the long rows of gas lamps. Street after street, where every-one lay asleep—street after street, all lit up as if for a procession, and all as empty as a church. At last, he got into that state of mind, when even a grown man listens and listens, and begins to long for the sight of a policeman.

All at once, he saw two figures. One was that of a little man who was walking at a good pace towards him on the opposite side of the road. The other was that of a girl of some ten or eleven years who was running as hard as she was able down a side street. To begin with, all Richard's attention was fastened on the girl. He wondered what a child of such tender years should be doing on the streets at this late hour, and at the way she ran, with her hair and her coat streaming out behind her, as if bound upon some urgent errand.

He saw what must happen next in the instant before it occurred. He opened his mouth to call a warning. He was too late. The child and the man ran into one another at the corner, almost beneath a lamp. The girl went down, with arms thrown wide and all the breath knocked out of her body. And then came the horrible part of the thing. The man trampled over the child's body, as if it was the most natural thing in the world, and left her screaming on the ground.

It sounds nothing to hear, perhaps, but it was a dreadful thing to see. It wasn't like the deed of a man at all—it was the action of a devil—a monster!

Richard swore. His hand tightened on his stick. The man was walking on without a backward glance, while behind him the scared and injured child lay screaming at the top of her voice.

Those screams had their effect. Along the street, someone threw open a window and called out to the child in an anxious voice. A moment later and other windows were being opened. It was clear that the girl would soon be given help and comfort. Richard made up his mind. He sprang across the street, after the man, with the speed of an angry cat.

He was, in spite of his size, very light on his feet, and he was almost upon the man before the fellow heard him coming. As he turned his head, Richard took him by the collar.

" One moment, my friend," he said grimly.

"I think you have some explaining to do."

The man turned, without haste. For a moment, while he stood looking up at Richard, and before he spoke, the young man felt a sudden chill, he was so struck by the shocking expression on the other's face. There was, he was sure, a glint of cruel satisfaction in the eyes. The face was in no way out of the ordinary; the dark hair grew rather low upon the forehead; the eyebrows were heavy and arched; the mouth large and full-lipped. But there was something in the eyes—something wicked and forbidding—some inner power that burned with a brilliant light. And the power was evil! Richard was sure of it! This man was bad, bad all through. There was something in him that filled Richard with disgust, so that he dropped his hand from the other's shoulder and muttered, scarcely conscious that he did so: "Ugh! filthy brute!"

The other was perfectly cool and had made no resistance, but now he gave Richard a look so ugly that it brought out the sweat on him as if he had been running.

"Your manners leave much to be desired, young fellow," said the man. He spoke with a whispering and somewhat broken voice. "Perhaps you will explain yourself."

"Explain myself!" cried Richard, losing all

patience. Really! The fellow's impudence passed all bounds. A feeling of hate went through him—he could not help himself—he lifted his stick. He had a longing to strike this man down, to rain blow after blow upon him, and his own feeling sickened him. " First," he continued in a rush of angry words, " perhaps *you* will explain your own beastly action in trampling upon that child and leaving her there upon the ground."

" That!" said the man calmly, and again Richard saw a glint of cruel satisfaction in his eyes. " *That*, my dear fellow, was nothing but an accident——"

" An accident!" said Richard hotly, almost choking upon the words. " Was it an accident that you walked over the girl—without a thought—or a glance—like a—a *machine*, rather than a man?"

Again, for an instant, that ugly look burned in the man's eyes; then his gaze passed beyond Richard, and his look showed something of fear. Richard swung round, and saw that a group of people had turned out of the neighbouring houses and were gathered around the child. Voices carried to them and, sounding above all, a man's sudden shout of anger. The child, it seemed, had told what had happened.

Richard smiled, grimly.

" You will be good enough to return," he said coldly, " to offer your sympathy and inquire what harm you may have done."

For a moment, the man hesitated. His eyes wandered over Richard's big frame, took in the broad shoulders and the determined set of the jaw. Then the eyes dropped, and the man nodded.

" Perhaps it would be as well," he said.

Without another word, the two set out towards the group under the lamp. There, in a ring, were a dozen or so men and women, only half dressed under the shabby coats they had pulled on when the child's screams had brought them from their beds. They stared suspiciously at Richard and his companion as the pair approached.

" Let me pass," said Richard quietly, and his evening dress and air of authority had their effect. The crowd opened, and the two moved into the circle.

The child lay still upon the ground, crying and trembling. But now her head was pillowed on the lap of a thin-faced woman who was kneeling beside her murmuring words of comfort. She, it seemed, was her mother. A short, wide-shouldered man with a large nose and thinning hair stood with his hand on the woman's shoulder, explaining to one of the bystanders what had happened.

" The wife's mother was taken queer,"
Richard heard him say, " and we sent young
Edie here to fetch the doctor. Then, all of a
sudden, we hears her scream—something horrible it was—turned me right over inside—and
we runs out and finds her here. She says," he
continued, as if he could not believe his own
words, " that a man knocked 'er down, and—
and just *walked over 'er!*"

The crowd muttered in a threatening manner.
Their eyes flashed and their faces, in the yellow
gaslight, particularly those of the women, had
a wild and savage look. The little man turned
as he became conscious of the presence of
Richard and his prisoner. Every eye was on
them now, except that of the sobbing child.

" I saw what happened," said Richard to
the little man, then nodded down at the girl.

" Is she badly hurt?"

" I don't think so," replied the man uncer-
tainly. " The doctor should be along in a
minute, an' we'll see. She's more shocked
than anything else, poor kid!"

He bent and patted the child's shoulder.
She lifted a dirty, tear-stained face and her
eyes, for some reason, went straight to the
face of the man at Richard's shoulder. They
widened and filled with fright. She gave a
scream.

"It's him!" she cried, and pointed. "He hurt me! Don't let him get me! Don't let him get me."

She buried her face in the woman's lap once more, clinging to her closely.

The child's father was staring at Richard's prisoner.

"Was it *you* that did it?" he asked in an astonished whisper.

"My good man, it was an accident——"

"An accident!" cried the father, and he was shaking with rage. He lifted a fist. "I'll accident *you!*" he exploded and started forward.

Richard heard the men behind him mutter, and one or two of them cursed.

"Give 'im something!" a rough voice cried.

"Knock 'is 'ead off!" a woman screamed.

It was an ugly moment. Richard found himself in the middle of a ring of angry faces—of men who cursed and threatened, of women who had their hands raised and their fingers curled as though ready to tear. . . The air was full of hate!

There came an unexpected interruption.

"What's all this?" cried a loud, deep voice, and a man in a dark coat and a high hat came shouldering his way through the crowd.

CHAPTER TWO

The Signature

THE crowd fell quiet at once and parted before the man to let him through. Here, quite clearly, was someone for whom they had much respect. Then Richard saw the black bag the man was carrying and knew at once who he was.

" Doctor Grant," cried the child's father eagerly. " Sir—it's our Edie. She's 'urt. Will you 'ave a look at 'er?"

His anger was forgotten, for the moment. All his thoughts were for his child. He led the doctor to her, and waited while a quick examination was made. The doctor rose and questioned the man in a low voice, the other answering and pointing from time to time at the man who stood so still and silent at Richard's side. While he waited, Richard passed his eye round the ring of staring faces and saw the expression of hate in everyone of them. It showed so clearly that it shocked him, and yet he knew that the same feeling was there in his own heart. He looked at his prisoner, who

9

was very conscious of that circle of hate, and yet who stood there, filled with a kind of black scorn—frightened, too, Richard could see—but carrying it all off like the Devil himself.

The doctor and the child's father were approaching them. The doctor was a tall, strong fellow with a brown beard.

" This is a bad business," he said, looking straight at the prisoner. " The child is not seriously hurt—but she's had a shock—a very bad shock—and it's hard to say what the consequences may be." He suddenly exploded into anger. " Devil take you, sir!" he cried. " If what I'm told is true, then you deserve to be whipped!"

Richard was struck immediately by the doctor's manner. As he looked at the prisoner, he turned sick and white with the desire to strike him down. Richard knew what was in his mind just as the doctor, after a glance at Richard, knew what was in his.

The prisoner had turned angry now.

" I've told you—the whole thing was an accident!" he said with extraordinary violence.

" I think it a matter for the police," answered the doctor, in a grim voice.

The crowd muttered their agreement. Now, Richard saw, there was a very worried look in

Next moment, he was trampling his victim beneath his feet. (Page 38)

the prisoner's eyes. A thought occurred to him; and it was one that pleased him.

" One moment," he said, " I am sure that Mr.—er—" he waved a hand towards the prisoner.

" Hyde," said the man, after a little hesitation. " Edward Hyde."

"—that Mr. Hyde wishes to avoid a scandal that would make him an object of contempt to the whole of London. Perhaps he would be willing to settle the matter without reference to the police, by expressing his sorrow for what has happened in the form of a gift of money to this poor girl's family."

Two or three who stood behind him applauded that. Mr. Hyde was very much aware of that change of feeling.

" If you choose to make capital of this accident," he said, " I am naturally helpless. I wish to avoid a scene. Name your figure."

Richard thought for a second. The man was a gentleman in dress and speech, if not in deed. He should be taught a lesson.

" Shall we say a hundred pounds?" asked Richard, gently.

Again the crowd muttered their approval. Mr. Hyde bit his lip, but nodded.

" Very well," he said. " I have neither cash nor cheque-book with me."

" You shall find one or the other," said Richard lightly, " and this gentleman"— indicating the child's father—" and I will keep you company until you have done so."

So it was arranged. In another moment or so, Mr. Hyde was leading Richard and the long-nosed man—who seemed greatly cheered at the thought of his hundred pounds—through the streets in the first pale light of morning. Not one of them said anything; they were all too busy with their thoughts.

They had walked for almost an hour, when Mr. Hyde turned into a quiet side street in a busy quarter of London. The street, though small, and in an unlovely neighbourhood, had a well-cared-for look, so that it shone out in the morning sunlight like a fire in a forest, with its freshly painted doors and windows, its well-polished brasses, and its general air of cleanliness.

Two doors from one corner, on the left hand going east, the line of neat houses was broken, however, by the opening into a little court. Just at that point, a certain sinister block of buildings hung forward over the street. It showed no window; nothing but a door on the ground level and a blind forehead of dirty wall above it. The door, which had neither bell nor knocker, was stained and unpainted, and looked as if it had not been opened for many years past.

It was before this door that Mr. Hyde came to a stop.

"If you will wait," he said, in his strangely broken voice, "I will enter and find you what you want."

The child's father started, and Richard saw a suspicious look enter the man's eyes. He put a hand on his arm.

"There will be no trickery," he told the man. "Mr. Hyde knows better, I am sure, than to attempt to fool us at this stage."

Hyde gave the pair of them a long, cold look, and curled his lip in scorn.

"You will be paid!" he said, in a voice like a dog's snarl, then took a key from his pocket and went into the house.

He returned in a matter of minutes with ten pounds in gold which he handed over to the child's father without a word. To Richard he handed a cheque.

"You had better deal with this," he said. "This fellow, as like as not, has no knowledge of such things, and will immediately suspect a trick."

Richard took the cheque and studied it. It was for the balance of the hundred pounds, to be drawn on Coutts's Bank, and made payable to bearer. So far, so good. But at sight of the signature, Richard stiffened, and looked up, a suspicious light in his own eyes. The cheque had been signed—Henry Jekyll; a name that Richard, and most of London, knew very well indeed. The great Dr. Jekyll was famous in the city, and his name was often in print. Could it be that the cheque was forged?

Mr. Hyde had read Richard's thoughts.

"Set your mind at rest," he said in his sneering way. "I will stay with you till the banks open, and cash the cheque myself."

Richard nodded.

"Perhaps it will be as well," he said, "if we go to my rooms, and wait there until the banks open."

Again, it was agreed. Richard managed to find a cab that carried them all to his rooms, where Mrs. Parker, his housekeeper, provided them with breakfast. When the time came, a second cab carried them to Coutts's Bank.

The three entered and waited, while Mr. Hyde presented the cheque at the counter. There could be no doubt that it was genuine. The money was paid in gold, and Mr. Hyde handed the bag containing it to the child's father, who took it in a kind of dream.

Mr. Hyde turned to Richard.

"I trust," he said, baring his teeth in that

snarling dog's way he had, " that you are satisfied with the part you have played in this affair. I shall know you, if we meet again."

He turned then, and walked away; watching him go, Richard felt once more that strong feeling of hate which the man seemed to stir in all whom he met. And it occurred to Richard then, for the first time, that in all that had passed Mr. Hyde had spoken no word of sorrow and shown no sign of pity for the terrible thing that he had done.

CHAPTER THREE

Blackmail House

M R. UTTERSON, the lawyer, was uncle to Richard Enfield. He was, to all appearances, a dry stick of a man, who owned a face that was seldom lit by a smile. He was long, lean, dull, and dusty— and yet somehow entirely lovable. At friendly meetings, and when the wine was to his taste, something very warm and human shone from his eye; something which never found its way into his talk, but showed itself more often in the deeds of his life.

In business he was known as a man who calculated every risk before he took action or gave advice; a cool man, a steady man, essentially a man of sense and authority. No one who had any association with him would have dreamed of suggesting that he could ever be guilty of wild flights of fancy or imagination; which lends greater weight, of course, to the evidence he has given in this strange and mysterious affair of Dr. Jekyll and Mr. Hyde . . .

The lawyer had known the good Dr. Jekyll for many years before he made the acquaintance of the evil Mr. Hyde; and it was through his nephew, Richard Enfield, that he heard tell of this wicked man before meeting him in the flesh.

It was the habit of Mr. Utterson and his nephew to walk together on Sunday afternoons. There were some people who could not understand what it was that these two saw in each other, or what subject they had in common. For all that, Richard had a great affection for the dry old lawyer, and both men looked upon their walks as occasions of pleasure, and even resisted the calls of business, that they might enjoy them uninterrupted.

It chanced on one of these excursions that their way led them into a rather dismal part of town, in which there stood one street of clean and neat little houses. Towards one corner, however, Mr. Utterson noticed an unpainted building that leaned forward over the entrance to a court.

As they drew level with this building, Mr. Enfield lifted his stick and pointed at its door.

'' Do you see that door?'' he asked. '' It is connected in my mind with a very odd story.''

'' Indeed!'' said Mr. Utterson, giving a start, and with a slight change of voice, '' and what was that?''

" It was this way," returned Mr. Enfield, as they moved on; and he went on to tell of the affair of the trampled child and the man who had showed no pity, without ever mentioning the names of Dr. Jekyll and Mr. Hyde.

Mr. Utterson heard him out in silence, though from time to time he made little sounds of sympathy or disgust.

" I see you feel as I do," said Mr. Enfield. " It's a bad story. My man was a fellow that no right-minded person would want anything to do with, if they could help it; and yet the man who signed the cheque is one of the most celebrated people in London. I suspect blackmail, you know; I'm afraid it's the case of an honest man paying heavily for some foolishness of his youth. Blackmail House is what I call that place, in consequence. Though even that doesn't explain it all," he added thoughtfully.

" And you don't know if the man who signed the cheque lives there?" asked Mr. Utterson, rather suddenly.

" He doesn't," returned Richard. " I happen to have noticed his address in one of the newspapers. He lives in some square or other, though I can't remember which."

" And you never made any inquiries about the other place?" asked Mr. Utterson.

" No—but I've studied the place for myself.

It seems to be hardly a house at all. There is no other door, and nobody goes in or out of the one we saw just now, except, occasionally, the gentleman of my adventure.''

For a while, the pair walked on in silence; and then—'' Richard,'' said Mr. Utterson, '' there's one point I want to ask: what is the name of the man who knocked down that child?''

'' Well,'' replied his nephew, '' I can't see what harm it would do to tell you. It was a man of the name of Hyde.''

'' H'm!'' said Mr. Utterson thoughtfully. '' What sort of man is he to see?''

'' He is not easy to describe. There is something wrong with his appearance—something hateful, and rather horrible. I never saw a man I so disliked, and yet I scarce know why. He gives a strong feeling of being deformed—but he is sound enough in body. It's as if there was something bad—something evil *inside*—which one can feel all the time one is near him. I noticed particularly how that doctor felt it, and when the fellow was in my rooms, I could see that he had the same effect on Mrs. Parker. I can't really describe him, however. And it's not for want of memory; in my mind's eye, I can see him at this very moment.''

Mr. Utterson walked some way in silence, clearly under a weight of consideration. "You are sure he used a key to enter that building?" he inquired at last. "You are *quite* sure?"

"My dear uncle . . ." began Richard, surprised out of himself.

"Yes, I know my question must seem strange," said Mr. Utterson, giving one of his rare, dry smiles. "I don't doubt that you are right, Richard. The fact is, I have heard something of this man Hyde before; I know what is behind the door he entered; and, if I do not ask you the name of the man who signed the cheque, it is because I know it already. It was Dr. Henry Jekyll, was it not?"

Richard stopped dead, and stared at his uncle with a look of complete astonishment.

"How on earth——" he began.

Mr. Utterson raised a hand to stop him, walked some yards without a word, his face very serious, and then——

"I can say no more at this time," he said. "The matter is confidential—you understand? —and I am already ashamed of my long tongue. But, believe me, Richard, something terrible is happening here among us in London; something terrible is happening—and there is worse to come!"

CHAPTER FOUR

Search for Mr. Hyde

HAT evening Mr. Utterson returned to his house in low spirits, and with little taste for the excellent dinner that was set before him. It was his custom of a Sunday, when this meal was over, to sit by the fire reading, until the clock of the neighbouring church rang out the hour of twelve, when he would go quietly and gratefully to bed.

On this night, however, as soon as the cloth was taken away, he took up a candle and went into his business room. There he opened his safe, took from the most private part of it an envelope that contained the will of Dr. Henry Jekyll, M.D., D.C.L., LL.D., F.R.S., etc., etc., and sat down to study its contents. The document was in the handwriting of Dr. Jekyll, for Mr. Utterson, though he had taken charge of it now that it was made, had refused to assist in the making of it. It provided that, in case of the death of Dr. Jekyll, all his possessions were to pass into the hands of his good friend Edward

Hyde; but that in case of Dr. Jekyll's " dis-appearance or unexplained absence for any period exceeding three calendar months ", the said Edward Hyde should step into the said Henry Jekyll's shoes without further delay.

This document had long been the lawyer's eyesore. It offended him both as a lawyer and as a lover of the sensible side of life, to whom the fanciful had little appeal. Beforehand, it had been his lack of knowledge of Mr. Hyde that had stirred his doubts and suspicions; now, by accident, it was what he had learned. It was bad enough when the man was only a name of which he could learn no more. It was worse when he began to be given shape, and the shape was evil . . .

" I thought, at first, that Jekyll was mad," he said, as he returned the document to the safe, " and now I begin to fear it is disgrace."

With that he blew out his candle, put on a greatcoat and set out for Cavendish Square, where his friend, the great Dr. Lanyon, had his house and received his patients. " If any-one knows, it will be Lanyon," he thought.

The servant led him from the door to the dining-room, where Dr. Lanyon sat alone over his wine. He was a healthy, red-faced gentle-man, with a head of snow-white hair and a noisy, decided manner. At sight of Mr. Utterson, he sprang up from his chair and welcomed him with both hands. These two were old friends, had known each other at school and college, and were men who thoroughly enjoyed each other's company.

After a little idle talk, the lawyer led up to the subject which so occupied his mind.

" I suppose, Lanyon," he said, " that you and I must be the two oldest friends that Henry Jekyll has?"

" I wish the friends were younger," said Dr. Lanyon, with a laugh. " Anyway, I see very little of Jekyll now."

" Indeed!" said Utterson. " I thought you shared a common interest."

" We did," was the reply. " But it is more than ten years since Henry Jekyll became too fanciful for me. He began to go wrong, wrong in mind; and though, of course, I continued to take an interest in him for old time's sake, I see and I have seen very little of him for a long time now. Such scientific rubbish," added the doctor, looking very angry, " I have never heard!"

This little show of temper was something of a relief to Mr. Utterson. " They have fallen out on some point of science," he thought; and being a man with no interest in science, he even added: " It is nothing worse than that!"

He gave his friend a few seconds to recover his good temper, and then approached the question he had come to put.

"Did you ever meet a friend of his—a Mr. Edward Hyde?" he asked.

"Hyde?" repeated Lanyon. "No. Never heard of him. Must be someone he's met since my time."

That was the amount of information that the lawyer carried back with him to his bed, on which he lay, anxious and wakeful, until the small hours of the morning. It was a night of little comfort to his uneasy mind, working in utter darkness, and asking questions to which he had no answer.

Six o'clock struck on the bells of the church that was so conveniently near to Mr. Utterson's home, and still he was digging at the problem. Until this time, it had been a problem of mind and reason; but now his imagination also was engaged, and as he turned from one side to the other in the darkness of the night and the curtained room, Mr. Enfield's story passed before his mind in a series of lighted pictures . . .

He was aware of the great field of lamps of a sleeping city; then of the figure of a man walking quickly; then of a child running from the doctor's; and then these met, and that monster in human form trampled the child underfoot and passed on regardless of her screams. Or else he would see a room in a rich house, where his friend lay asleep, dreaming and smiling at his dreams; and then the door of that room would be opened, the curtains of the bed pulled apart, and there would stand by his side a figure that had no face, but whose hand pointed with a threatening gesture, and that compelled the sleeper to wake and rise and follow it . . .

That figure troubled the lawyer all night through; and if at any time he fell into a light sleep, it was only to see it move slowly among sleeping houses, or move more quickly, then faster still, to great speed, through wider avenues of a lamp-lighted city; and at every street corner trample over a child and leave her screaming. And still the figure had no face by which he might know it—or only one that was there for but an instant and melted before his eyes.

And thus it was that there sprang up and grew in the lawyer's mind a strong curiosity to see the face of the real Mr. Hyde. If he could but once set eyes on him, he thought, the mystery would lighten and perhaps roll away altogether, as was the habit of mysterious things when well examined. He might find a reason for his friend's preference, and even for the unusual conditions of the will. And, at least, it would be a face worth seeing: the face of a man who had no mercy or pity in him; a face which had but to show itself to raise up in the mind of Mr. Enfield a spirit of lasting hatred.

From that time forward, Mr. Utterson began to haunt the door in the side street where he had walked with Mr. Enfield. In the morning before office hours, in the middle of the day when business was plenty and time scarce, at night under the face of the moon, by all lights and at all hours, the lawyer was to be found at his chosen post.

And at last his patience was rewarded.

It was a fine dry night, cold and clear; the streets were as clean as a dance room floor; the lamps, unshaken by any wind, threw a regular pattern of light and shadow. By ten o'clock, when the shops were closed, the street was very solitary, and, in spite of the low noises of London from all around, very silent. Small sounds carried far; and the approach of any traveller was signalled by the noise of steps that went before him. Mr. Utterson had been some minutes at his post when he was aware of an odd, light footstep drawing near. In the course of his nightly watches, he had long grown accustomed to the odd effect by which the footfalls of a single person, while he is still

a great way off, suddenly spring out distinct
from the hum of the great city. Yet his attention was immediately arrested; and it was
with a strong feeling of success, at last, that he
drew back into the shelter of the court.

The steps drew nearer and swelled out,
suddenly louder, as they turned the end of the
street. The lawyer, peeping out, could soon
see what manner of man he had to deal with.
He was small, and very plainly dressed; and
the look of him, even at that distance, somehow
filled the watcher with dislike. The man made
straight for the door, in a great hurry; and as
he came, he drew a key from his pocket, like
one approaching home.

Mr. Utterson stepped out and touched him on
the shoulder as he passed. "Mr. Hyde, I think?"

Mr. Hyde drew back, giving a low cry. His
fear lasted an instant only; and though he did
not look the lawyer in the face, he answered
coolly enough: "That is my name. What do
you want?"

"I see you are going in," returned the
lawyer. "I am an old friend of Dr. Jekyll's—
my name is Utterson—you must have heard
Jekyll mention it; and meeting you so conveniently I thought you might admit me. I
know, you see, that this door is a back way to
Jekyll's laboratory."

" You will not find Dr. Jekyll; he is from home," replied Mr. Hyde. And then suddenly, but still without looking up, " How did you know me?" he asked.

Mr. Utterson avoided the question.

" Tell me," he said, " will you do me a favour?"

" With pleasure," replied the other. " What shall it be?"

" Will you let me see your face?" asked the lawyer.

Mr. Hyde appeared to hesitate. And then, as if upon some sudden reflection, and with a strange air of daring, he looked up, and the pair stared at each other for a few seconds.

" Now I shall know you again," said Mr. Utterson. " It may be useful."

" Yes," returned Mr. Hyde, " it is as well we have met; and you should have my address, I think."

He gave the number of a street in Soho.

" Good God!" thought Mr. Utterson, " can he too have been thinking of the will?" But he kept his feelings to himself, and only nodded his thanks for the address.

" And now," said the other, " how did you know me?"

" By description," was the reply.

" Whose description?"

" We have common friends," said Mr. Utterson.

" Common friends!" echoed Mr. Hyde, as if astonished. " Who are they?"

" Jekyll, for instance," said the lawyer.

" He never told you," cried Mr. Hyde, angrily. " I see you are a liar!"

" Come," said Mr. Utterson, " that is not fitting language."

The other gave a kind of savage, snarling laugh; and the next moment, with extreme quickness, he had unlocked the door and vanished into the house.

CHAPTER FIVE

Dr. Jekyll

THE lawyer stood for the space of two minutes when Mr. Hyde had left him, the very picture of anxiety. Then he began to walk slowly along the street, pausing every step or two, and lifting a hand to his head like a man who is trying to puzzle out a problem. It was a problem that could not be easily solved . . .

Mr. Hyde was short and pale; he gave one the feeling that he was deformed, and yet was sound of body; he had an ugly smile; he had carried himself with a strange mixture of the timid and the daring; and he spoke with a whispering and somewhat broken voice—all these were points against him, but not all of these together could explain the disgust, dislike and fear with which Mr. Utterson now regarded him.

" There must be something else," said the puzzled gentleman. " There *is* something more, if I could find a name for it. God bless me, the man seems hardly human—he is a kind

of *monster!* Can it be that there is something so
foul inside him that it has an effect upon the
man's appearance? Oh, my poor old Harry
Jekyll, if ever I read the Devil's mark upon a
face, it is on that of your new friend!''

Round the corner from the side street there
was a square of ancient, well-built houses. Mr.
Utterson stopped at the door of the one that
stood second from the corner, which wore a
great air of wealth and comfort, and rang the
bell. A well-dressed servant opened the door.

'' Is Dr. Jekyll at home, Poole?'' asked the
lawyer.

'' I will see, Mr. Utterson,'' said Poole,
admitting the visitor into a large, low-roofed,
comfortable hall, warmed by a bright open
fire, and furnished in a costly manner. '' Will
you wait by the fire, sir, or shall I give you
a light in the dining-room?''

'' Here, thank you,'' said the lawyer, drawing close to the fire. This hall, in which he was
left alone, was a pet fancy of his friend the
doctor's; and Utterson himself always thought
of it as the most pleasant room in London. But
tonight there seemed a coldness in his blood;
the face of Hyde sat heavy on his memory; he
seemed to have no enthusiasm for life; and
could read a kind of threat in the dancing of the
firelight on the polished furniture and the

uneasy starting of the shadows on the roof. He was ashamed of his relief when Poole presently returned to announce that Dr. Jekyll was out.

" I saw Mr. Hyde go in by the laboratory door, Poole," he said. " Is that right, when Dr. Jekyll is from home?"

" Quite right, Mr. Utterson," replied the servant. " Mr. Hyde has a key."

" Your master seems to place a great deal of trust in that young man, Poole," said the other, thoughtfully.

" Yes, sir, he does indeed," said Poole. " We all have orders to obey him."

" I do not think I ever met Mr. Hyde," said Utterson.

" Oh, dear no, sir. He never *dines* here," replied the servant. " Indeed, we see very little of him on this side of the house. He usually comes and goes by the laboratory door."

" Well, good night, Poole."

" Good night, Mr. Utterson."

And the lawyer set out for home with a very heavy heart.

" Poor Harry Jekyll," he thought. " He is mixed up in something that will surely do him harm. He was wild when he was young—and perhaps Mr. Hyde has knowledge of some old sin. It *must* be that! He is a blackmailer, I am sure." And then suddenly there occurred an idea that gave him new hope. "If this Mr. Hyde were studied," he thought, "he must have secrets of his own; black secrets, by the look of him; secrets, compared to which, poor Jekyll's worst would be like sunshine. Things cannot continue as they are. It turns me cold to think of this creature stealing like a thief to Harry's bedside. And the danger of it! For if this Hyde suspects the existence of the will, he may grow impatient and hasten Harry's death. I am sure that he would not stop at murder, if it served his purpose. I must do something about all this—if Jekyll will let me—if Jekyll will only let me!"

And, as he walked, he saw once more before his eyes the strange conditions of the will.

.   .   .   .

A fortnight later, by excellent good fortune, the doctor gave one of his pleasant dinners to some five or six old friends, all intelligent men of the very best reputation, and all judges of good wine; and Mr. Utterson so managed that he stayed behind after the others had departed. This was no new arrangement, but a thing that had happened many times before. Where Utterson was liked, he was liked well. Hosts loved to detain the dry lawyer, when the light-hearted and the loose-tongued had left them; they liked to sit for a while in the man's rich silence,

after the expense and strain of gaiety. To this
rule Dr. Jekyll was no exception; and as he
sat now on the opposite side of the fire—a large,
well-made, smooth-faced man of fifty—you
could see by his looks that he had for Mr.
Utterson a sincere and warm affection.

"I have been wanting to speak to you,
Jekyll," began the lawyer. "You know that
will of yours?"

A close observer might have gathered that
the topic was not one that the doctor wished
to discuss at that time; but he carried it off
gaily enough.

"My poor Utterson," he smiled, "you are
unlucky to have such a client. I never saw a
man so worried as you were by my will; unless
it was that stupid fellow, Lanyon, at what he
called my scientific *rubbish*! Oh, I know he's a
good fellow—you needn't look upset—an excellent fellow, and I always mean to see more
of him, but he's no true scientist, for all that.
I was never more disappointed in any man than
in Lanyon."

"You know that I never approved of it,"
said Utterson, paying no regard to the fresh
topic.

"My will? Yes, certainly, I know that," said
the doctor, rather sharply. "You have told
me so."

" Well, I tell you so again," continued the lawyer. " I have been learning something of young Hyde."

The large, good-looking face of Dr. Jekyll grew pale to the very lips, and there came a blackness about his eyes. " I do not care to hear more," he said sharply.

" What I heard was bad—*very* bad!" said Utterson.

" It can make no change. You do not understand my position," returned the doctor, in a rather wild manner. " I am painfully placed, Utterson; my position is a very strange one. It is one of those affairs that cannot be mended by talking."

" Jekyll," said Utterson, " you know me. I am a man to be trusted. Tell me in confidence what is wrong—and I should not be at all surprised if I can get you out of it."

" My good Utterson," replied the doctor, " this is very good of you, and I cannot find words to thank you. I believe you, and I would trust you before any man alive—before myself, if I could make the choice; but indeed it isn't what you fancy; it is not so bad as that; and just to put your good heart at rest, I will tell you one thing: the moment I choose, I can be rid of Mr. Hyde. I give my hand upon that; and I thank you again and again. And I will just add one little word, Utterson, that I'm sure you'll take in the right spirit—this is a private matter, and I beg you to let it sleep.''

Utterson reflected a little, looking into the fire.

'' I have no doubt you are perfectly right,'' he said at last, getting to his feet.

'' But since we have touched upon this business, and for the last time, I hope,'' continued the doctor, '' there is one point I should like you to understand. I have really a very great interest in poor Hyde. I know you have seen him; he told me so; and I fear he was rude. But I do sincerely take a great, a very great, interest in that young man; and if I am taken away, Utterson, I wish you to promise me that you will bear with him and get his rights for him. I think you would, if you knew all; and it would be a weight off my mind if you would promise.''

'' I can't pretend that I shall ever like him,'' said the lawyer.

'' I don't ask that,'' said Jekyll gently, laying his hand on the other's arm. '' I only ask for justice. I only ask you to help him for my sake, when I am no longer here.''

Utterson nodded.

'' Very well,'' he said quietly, '' I promise.''

CHAPTER SIX

The Carew Murder Case

NEARLY a year later, in the month of October 18—, all London was shocked by a crime—a particularly fierce and cruel murder — that received all the more publicity because of the high position of the victim. The details were few and surprising in themselves. A maidservant living alone in a house not far from the river had gone upstairs to bed about eleven. Although a fog rolled over the city in the small hours, the early part of the night was cloudless, and the lane, which the maid's window overlooked, was brilliantly lit by the full moon. It seems that she enjoyed the moonlight, for she sat down upon a chair which stood immediately under the window, and fell into a kind of waking dream. Never (she used to say, her eyes full of tears, when she told of that experience), never had she felt more at peace with all men or thought more kindly of the world.

As she sat, she became aware of a white-

haired old gentleman drawing near the lane;
and advancing to meet him, another smaller
gentleman, to whom at first she paid less attention. When they had come within speaking
distance (which was just under the maid's
window) the old man greeted the other in a
polite and friendly manner. It did not seem as
if the subject of his address were of great
importance; indeed, from his pointing, it
appeared as if he were only inquiring his way;
but the moon shone on his face as he spoke, and
the girl was pleased to watch it, since the old
man wore such an air of innocence and self-
content. Presently her eyes wandered to the
other, and she was surprised to recognize in
him a certain Mr. Hyde, who had once visited
her master, and to whom she had taken a
strong dislike. He had in his hand a heavy
walking-stick, with which he kept tapping the
ground; but he seemed not to answer, and to
listen with an ill-contained impatience. And
then, all of a sudden he broke out in a great
flame of anger, stamped with his foot, lifted
the stick, and began shouting like a madman.
The old gentleman took a step back, with the
look of one very much surprised and hurt; and
at that Mr. Hyde seemed to lose all control of
himself, and struck the old man to the earth.
Next moment, he was trampling his victim

beneath his feet, raining down a storm of blows, under which the bones could be heard breaking. At the horror of these sights and sounds the maid fainted.

It was two o'clock when she came to herself and called for the police. The murderer was gone long since; but there lay his victim in the middle of the lane. The stick with which the deed had been done, although it was of some rare and very tough and heavy wood, had broken in the middle, for one half still lay in the road—the other, without doubt, had been carried away by the murderer. A purse and a gold watch were found upon the victim; but neither cards nor papers except a stamped envelope, which he had probably been carrying to the post, and which bore the name and address of Mr. Utterson.

This was brought to the lawyer the next morning, before he was out of bed; and he had no sooner seen it, and been told the circumstances, than he looked very solemn. "I shall say nothing till I have seen the body," he said. "This may be very serious. Have the kindness to wait while I dress." And with the same solemn face he hurried through his breakfast and drove to the police station, where the body had been carried. As soon as he came into the cell, he nodded,

"Yes," he said, "I recognize him. I am sorry to say that this is Sir Danvers Carew."

"Good God, sir!" cried the officer, "is it possible?" And the next moment his eye lighted up with professional ambition. "This will make a great deal of noise," he said. "Perhaps you can help us find the man."

In a brief way, he told what the maid had seen, and showed the broken stick.

Mr. Utterson had already paled at the name of Hyde; but when the stick was laid before him, he could doubt no longer; broken as it was, he recognized it as one that he had himself presented many years before to Henry Jekyll.

"Is this Mr. Hyde a small person?" he inquired.

"Particularly small and particularly wicked looking, is what the maid calls him," said the officer.

Mr. Utterson thought for some moments, and then, raising his head, "If you will come with me in my cab," he said, "I think I can take you to his house."

It was by this time about nine in the morning, and the first fog of the season had fallen over London. As the cab crawled from street to street in the half-light, the dismal quarter of Soho, with its muddy ways and dirty people, its feeble lamps and filthy shops, seemed, in the

lawyer's eyes, like a district of some city in a
nightmare. The thoughts of his mind were as
dark and sad as the day itself; and when he
glanced at the companion of his drive, he was
conscious of some touch of that terror of the
law and the law's officers which may at all
times visit the most honest among us.

As the cab drew up before the address he had
given, the fog lifted a little and showed him a
dirty little street of mean and dismal houses.
This was the home of Henry Jekyll's friend; of
a man who was heir to a quarter of a million
pounds.

An old woman with silver hair opened the
door. She had an evil face and eyes that were
set too close together, but her manners were
excellent. Yes, she said, this was Mr. Hyde's,
but he was not at home; he had come in that
night very late, but he had gone away again in
less than an hour; there was nothing strange
in that; he was often absent—for instance, it
was nearly two months since she had seen him
till yesterday.

" Very well, then, we wish to see his rooms,"
said the lawyer; and when the woman began
to declare it was impossible, " I had better tell
you who this person is," he added. " This is
Inspector Newcomen, of Scotland Yard."

A look of joy appeared upon the woman's

face. "Ah!" said she, with evident satisfaction, "Mr. Hyde is in trouble! What has he done?"

Mr. Utterson and the inspector exchanged glances.

"He doesn't seem a very popular character," said the inspector. "And now, my good woman, just let me and this gentleman have a look about us."

In the whole extent of the house, which but for the old woman remained otherwise empty, Mr. Hyde had used only a couple of rooms; but these were furnished in the best of taste. There was a well-stocked wine cupboard; the plate was of silver; a good picture hung upon the walls, a gift (as Utterson supposed) from Henry Jekyll, who had a fine feeling for such things; and the carpets were of the finest quality. At this moment, however, the rooms bore every mark of having been turned upside down; clothes lay about the floor, with their pockets inside out; drawers stood pulled open; and in the fireplace there lay a pile of grey ashes, as though many papers had been burned. From these ashes the inspector dug out the stub end of a green cheque-book which had resisted the action of the fire; the other half of the stick was found behind the door; and as this turned suspicion into a certain fact, the officer declared himself delighted. A visit to the bank, where several thousand pounds were found to be lying in the murderer's name, completed his satisfaction.

"You may depend on it, sir," he told Mr. Utterson, "I have him in my hand. He must have lost his head, or he never would have left the stick, or, above all, burned the cheque-book. Why, money is life to the man. We have nothing to do but wait for him at the bank, and seize him when he arrives."

This last, however, was easier said than done. Mr. Hyde did not appear at the bank. He had few friends—even the employer of the maid-servant had only seen him twice; his family could nowhere be found; he had never been photographed; and the few who could describe him held very different opinions as to his looks. Only on one point were they agreed—that was the odd way in which Hyde gave the sense of being deformed. This was something that had struck them all.

CHAPTER SEVEN

The Letter

*I*T was late in the afternoon of that same day when Mr. Utterson found his way to Dr. Jekyll's door. He was at once admitted by Poole, and led down by the kitchen and across a yard which had once been a garden, to the building where the doctor had his laboratory. It was the first time that the lawyer had been received in that part of his friend's quarters, and he looked around him with curiosity, at the tables and shelves with their load of chemicals and equipment.

At the farther end, a flight of stairs rose to a door, and through this Mr. Utterson was at last received into the doctor's study. It was a large room, fitted with bookshelves, furnished among other things with a long narrow mirror and a business table, and looking out upon the court by three dusty windows barred with iron. A cheerful fire was burning; a lamp was set lighted upon the chimney shelf, for even in the houses the fog began to lie thickly; and there, close up to the warmth, sat Dr. Jekyll, looking ill and white as paper. He did not rise to meet his visitor, but held out a cold hand, and welcomed him in a voice that shook.

" And now," said Mr. Utterson, as soon as Poole had left them, " you have heard the news?"

The doctor was trembling violently. He nodded.

" The newsboys were crying it in the square," he said. " I heard them in my dining-room."

" One word," said the lawyer. " Carew was my client, but so are you; and I want to know what I am doing. You have not been mad enough to hide this fellow from the police?"

" I swear to God," cried the doctor, " that I will never set eyes on him again. I am done with him in this world. It is all at an end. And, indeed, he does not want my help. You do not know him as I do; he is safe, he is quite safe; mark my words, he will never be heard of again."

The lawyer listened with a gloomy face. He did not like his friend's feverish manner.

" You seem pretty sure of him," he said, " and for your sake, I hope you are right. If it came to a trial, your name might appear."

" I am quite sure of him," replied Jekyll. " I have reasons for being certain that I cannot share with anyone. But there is one thing on which you may advise me. I have—I have received a letter, and I do not know whether I should show it to the police. I should like to leave it in your hands, Utterson. You will judge wisely, I am sure. I have so great a trust in you."

" You fear, I suppose, that it may help the police to find him?" asked the lawyer.

" No," said the other. ' I cannot say that I care what becomes of Hyde; I am quite done with him. I was thinking of my own character, which this terrible business has rather exposed."

Utterson reflected for a while; he was surprised at his friend's selfishness, and yet relieved by it.

" Well," he said at last, " let me see the letter."

The letter was written in an odd, back-sloping hand, and signed " Edward Hyde ". It stated, briefly enough, that the writer's good friend Dr. Jekyll, whose generosity he had so badly repaid, need have no fears for his safety, as he had means of escape on which he could depend beyond any shadow of doubt.

The letter filled Mr. Utterson with a great relief. It put a better colour on the friendship

than he had looked for, and he blamed himself
for some of his past suspicions.

" Have you the envelope?" he asked.

" I burned it," replied Jekyll, " before I
thought what I was about. But it bore no post-
mark. The note was handed in at my door."

" Shall I keep this, and think upon it?"
asked Utterson.

" I wish you to judge for me entirely," was
the reply. ' I have lost confidence in myself."

" Well, I shall consider," returned the
lawyer. " And now one thing more: was it
Hyde who dictated the terms in your will about
that disappearance?"

The doctor seemed seized with an attack of
fever, his hands shook so much. Then he shut
his mouth tight and nodded.

" I knew it!" said Utterson, with satisfaction. " He meant to murder you. You have
had a lucky escape!"

" I have had what is far more to the purpose,"
returned the doctor in a solemn voice; " I
have had a lesson—Oh, God, Utterson, what a
lesson I have had!"

He covered his face for a moment with his
hands.

On his way out, the lawyer stopped and had
a word or two with Poole.

" I believe there was a letter handed in

today," he said.   " What was the messenger
like?"

Poole was quite certain that nothing had
come except by post; " and only bills even
then, sir," he added.

This news sent off the visitor with all his
fears returned. Plainly the letter had come by
the laboratory door, he tried to tell himself;
possibly, indeed, it had been written in the
study. If that were so, it must be differently
judged, and handled with all the more caution.

As he felt his way through the fog, the newsboys were shouting all along the footways:
" Special edition! Shocking murder of M.P."
That told of the end of one friend and client;
and he could not help fearing that the good
name of another might suffer in the scandal. It
was, at the least, a difficult decision that he had
to make; and he began to feel a strong desire
for advice, which was not his way at all.

Soon after, he sat on one side of his own
fireplace, with Mr. Guest, his head clerk, upon
the other, and between them, at a carefully
calculated distance from the fire, a bottle of a
particular old wine that he had long kept for
some special occasion. The fog still hung over
the drowned city, where the lamps shone with
but a feeble glow; and through the thickness
of these fallen clouds, the processions of the

town's life were still rolling in by the great roads with a sound as of a mighty wind.

The room, however, was gay with firelight, and by degrees the lawyer's spirits rose. There was no man from whom he kept fewer secrets than Mr. Guest; and he was not always sure that he kept as many as he meant. Guest had often been on business to the doctor's. He knew Poole. He could scarce have failed to hear of Mr. Hyde's familiarity about the house. He might have ideas of his own; was it not right, then, that he should see a letter which put the mystery to rights, as far as Dr. Jekyll was concerned? Also, and above all, since Guest was a great student and critic of handwriting, he would consider the step a natural one. The clerk, besides, was a man of wise counsel; he would scarce read so strange a document without dropping a remark; and by that remark Mr. Utterson might shape his future course.

" This is a sad business about Sir Danvers," he said.

" Yes, sir, indeed. It has stirred up a very strong public feeling," returned Guest. " The murderer, of course, was a madman."

" I should like to hear your views on that," replied Utterson. " I have a note here in his handwriting. It is between ourselves, for I scarce know what to do about it; it is an ugly business at the best. But there it is—something that will interest you—the handwriting and signature of a murderer!''

Guest's eyes grew bright, and he sat down at once and studied the note closely.

'' No, sir,'' he said, '' not mad—but it is an odd hand.''

'' And by all accounts a very odd writer,'' added the lawyer.

Just then the servant entered with a note.

'' Is that from Dr. Jekyll, sir?'' inquired the clerk. '' I thought I knew the writing. Anying private, Mr. Utterson?''

'' Only an invitation to dinner. Why? Do you want to see it?''

'' For one moment. I thank you, sir.''

The clerk laid the two sheets of paper side by side and compared their contents.

'' Thank you, sir,'' he said at last, returning both. '' It's a very interesting signature.''

There was a pause, during which Mr. Utterson struggled with himself.

'' Why did you compare them, Guest?'' he asked suddenly.

'' Well, sir,'' replied the clerk, '' there's a rather odd likeness. The two hands are in many points the same—only differently sloped.''

'' Rather odd,'' said Utterson.

" Yes, sir—rather odd," returned Guest.

" I wouldn't speak of this note, you know," said his master.

" No, sir," said the clerk. " I understand."

But no sooner was Mr. Utterson alone that night than he locked the note in his safe, where it remained from that time forward.

" What!" he thought. " Henry Jekyll forge for a murderer!"

It was a thought that made his blood run cold.

CHAPTER EIGHT

The Terror of Doctor Lanyon

IME ran on. Thousands of pounds were offered as reward for the capture of Mr. Hyde, since the death of Sir Danvers was looked upon as a public injury. The murderer, however, had vanished as completely as if he had never existed. Much of his past was unearthed, indeed, and all of it was bad; tales came out of the man's violence and cruelty, of his evil life and ways, of his strange associates, of the hatred that seemed to have surrounded his career; but of his present whereabouts not a whisper. From the time he had left the house in Soho on the morning of the murder, he had been seen by no one.

Gradually, as time drew on, Mr. Utterson began to recover what he liked to call his '' sense of balance '', and to feel more at peace with himself and the world. The death of Sir Danvers was, to his way of thinking, more than paid for by the disappearance of Mr. Hyde. Now that the evil influence had vanished from his

home, a new life began for Dr. Jekyll. He gave
up his solitary life and began to go out into the
world once more. He invited all his old friends
into his home and became their familiar guest
and entertainer. While he had always been
known as a good and a generous man, he was
now no less distinguished for religion. He was
busy, he was much in the open air, he did good;
his face seemed to open and brighten, and for
more than two months the doctor was at
peace.

On the 8th of January, Utterson had dined
at the doctor's with a small party. Lanyon had
been there, and had seemed to enjoy the company of his old friend, Jekyll. On the 12th, and
again on the 14th, Jekyll's door was shut
against the lawyer.

"The doctor is busy in his laboratory,"
Poole said, "and is unable to see anyone."

On the 15th Utterson tried again, and was
again refused. Having grown used to seeing his
friend almost daily, the lawyer was worried by
this change of attitude. He went, therefore, to
Dr. Lanyon's to see what he knew of Jekyll's
return to the solitary life.

There, at least, he was not denied admit-
tance; but when he came in, he was shocked
at the change which had taken place in the
doctor's appearance. The healthy, red-faced

man had grown pale; he looked old and very tired, and moved feebly as if the will to live had left him. But it was his eyes that left the lawyer badly shocked. They were *frightened* eyes, eyes that seemed to show and reveal some deep-seated terror of the mind.

When Utterson spoke to the doctor of his ill looks, Lanyon declared himself to be a man at death's door.

"I am a doctor," he said, and his voice had lost its old certainty and firmness, "and I know that my days are numbered."

"Jekyll is ill, too," said Utterson. "Have you seen him?"

Lanyon's face changed. He grew as white as paper, and that look of terror became very clear to see. He held up a hand that trembled.

"I don't wish to see or hear any more of Dr. Jekyll," he said. "I am quite finished with him—and I beg that you will not mention his name in this house. As far as I am concerned, he is dead already, and better forgotten!"

"Tut, tut!" said Utterson, astonished; and then, after a long pause: "Isn't there anything I can do?" he asked. "We are three very old friends, Lanyon, and we're too old to make new ones."

"I will never see him again," said Lanyon.

" He knows that—and he knows why. Why
don't you ask him?"

" He won't see me," replied the lawyer.

" I am not surprised," said Lanyon. " Some
day, after I am dead, you may perhaps come to
learn the right and wrong of this. I can't tell
you now. But, in the meantime, if you can sit
and talk to me of other things, for God's sake
do so! If you *must* speak of Jekyll, however,
then, in God's name, go, for I cannot bear it."

As soon as he got home, Utterson sat down
and wrote to Jekyll, complaining of the way
his door had been shut against him, and asking
the cause of this unhappy break with Lanyon.
The next day brought him a long answer, that
did nothing to throw light on the mystery. The
quarrel with Lanyon, it seemed, was something
which no one could cure.

" I do not blame our old friend," Jekyll
wrote, " but I share his view that we must
never meet again. I mean, from this time on,
to shut myself away from the world. You must
not be surprised, nor must you doubt my friendship, if my door is often shut even to you. You
must let me go my own, dark way. I have
brought on myself a danger and a punishment
that I cannot name. If I am the chief of sinners,
I am the chief of sufferers also. I did not know,
indeed, that this world contained a place for

such sufferings and terrors as I have known;
and these are things that I have brought upon
my own head. If you wish to help me, Utterson,
you can do but one thing—and that is to leave
me to go my own way.''

Utterson was astonished.   After the dark
influence of Hyde had been taken from him, the
doctor had returned to his old friends. A week
ago, all had been well with him.   Now, in a
moment, all that was wrecked.   So great a
change pointed to madness, the lawyer thought,
but in view of Lanyon's words and manner
there must be some deeper reason.

A week later Dr. Lanyon took to his bed.
He never left it again, and in less than a fortnight he was dead.

The night after the funeral, Utterson locked
the door of his business room and, sitting there
by the light of a candle he drew out and set
before him an envelope addressed by the hand
of his dead friend, and marked: '' PRIVATE:
for the hands of J. C. Utterson ALONE, and, in
the event of his death, *to be destroyed unread*.''

Utterson sat there and looked at it for a
long time.   Here, perhaps, was the key to the
mystery.   He was afraid to open it, however.

'' I have buried one friend today,'' he
thought.   '' What if this should cost me
another?''

And then he dismissed the fear, and tore the envelope open. Inside was a second envelope, marked upon the cover as '' not to be opened till the death or disappearance of Dr. Henry Jekyll ''.

Utterson could hardly believe his eyes. Here was that word '' disappearance '' once more, as in the mad will, which he had long ago returned to Jekyll. The will, Utterson was sure, had been made at the sinister suggestion of the man Hyde, for an evil and horrible purpose of his own. But there was the same idea written by the hand of Lanyon.

What could it mean? The lawyer was seized by a great curiosity; he felt a temptation to tear open the envelope and dive at once to the bottom of these mysteries. His professional honour and faith to his dead friend would not permit him to do so, however. He rose, at last, and placed the packet in his private safe.

But he could not shut away his curiosity. From that time on, he wished more than ever to see and speak with Jekyll. He went to call, again and again; and always he had the same answer. He spoke with Poole upon the door-step, and learned that the doctor now shut himself more than ever in his study or the laboratory, where he would sometimes even sleep. He was out of spirits, he had grown very silent, he did not read, and it seemed as if something was preying on his mind.

Utterson grew so used to these reports that, in the end, he gave up calling altogether. When, at last, he did set eyes on Jekyll once more, it was in circumstances that only added to the mystery, and left Mr. Utterson himself badly shaken. . . .

Jekyll gave one cry, and started to his feet, his hand at his throat.
(Page 61)

CHAPTER NINE

The Face at the Window

*I*T chanced one Sunday, when Mr. Utterson was on his usual walk with Richard Enfield, that their way lay once again through the side street in which stood the house with *the door*. When they came in front of that door, both stopped to look at it.

" Well," said Enfield at last, " that story's at an end. We shall see no more of Mr. Hyde."

" I hope not," said Utterson. " Did I ever tell you that I once saw him, and shared your feeling of disgust?"

" It was impossible to do the one without the other," returned Enfield. " And, by the way, what a fool you must have thought me, not to know that this door was a back way to Dr. Jekyll's laboratory."

" So you found it out, did you?" said Utterson. " But, if you *do* know, we may as well step into the court and take a look at the windows. To tell you the truth, I'm very uneasy about poor Jekyll. It might do him good if he sees a friend, even outside."

The court was very cool and a little damp. Shut in as it was, it was also rather dark, although the sky, high up overhead, was still bright with sunset. There were three windows in the wall of Jekyll's laboratory building, and the middle one was half open. Sitting close beside it, his face sad and gloomy—almost like a prisoner, thought Utterson—was Dr. Jekyll himself.

" Hullo, Jekyll!" the lawyer cried.   " I trust that you are better."

Jekyll lifted a hand.

" I am very low, Utterson," he replied, " very low. It will not last long, thank God."

" You stay too much indoors," said the lawyer.   " You should be out in the air, like Enfield and me.   This is my nephew.   Mr. Enfield—Dr. Jekyll.   Come on now, get your hat and take a walk with us.   It will do you good."

" It's very kind of you," returned Jekyll, " and I should like to very much—but no, it is quite impossible.   I dare not!   All the same, I am very glad to see you, Utterson; this is really a great pleasure.   I would ask you and Mr. Enfield up, but the place is really not fit."

" Well, then," said the lawyer, in his good-natured way, " the best thing we can do is to stay down here, and speak with you from where we are.''

'' That is just what I was going to suggest,'' returned the doctor, with a smile.

The words had hardly left his lips, when the smile was struck from his face. His eyes grew suddenly large with fear. His face took on a look of such terror and despair, as froze the blood of the gentlemen below. And then, before their eyes, the face seemed to blacken, to twist and alter and melt before their eyes, becoming something different, something horrible and frightening . . .

They had only a glimpse, however. Jekyll gave one cry, and started to his feet, his hand at his throat. The window was instantly closed, and the doctor passed from sight . . .

That glimpse had been sufficient. The two turned and left the court without a word. It was not until they had turned into another street, where people were passing to and fro, that Mr. Utterson turned and looked at his companion. They were both pale; and there was an answering horror in their eyes.

'' God forgive us!'' said Mr. Enfield softly.

But Mr. Utterson only nodded his head very seriously, and they walked on once more in silence.

CHAPTER TEN

The Last Night

M R. UTTERSON was sitting by his fire on a night in March, a bottle of good wine close to hand, when he heard the front door-bell ring. A minute later Jekyll's servant, Poole, was shown into the room.

" Bless me, Poole, what brings you here?" cried the lawyer; and then, taking a second look at the man's face, " What's wrong?" he added. " Is the doctor ill?"

" Mr. Utterson," said the man, " there's something wrong."

The lawyer came to his feet.

" Here, take a chair," he said, " and let me pour you a glass of wine. Now, sit down, take your time, and tell me what you want."

Poole sank into a chair, and took a glass of wine like a man in a dream. His hand shook, the wine spilled, but he did not seem to see it.

" Now, Poole," said the lawyer, firmly.

" Sir," said Poole, " you know how the doctor's been for some time now, and how he shuts himself up. Well, he's shut up again in the laboratory, and I don't like it, sir. Mr. Utterson, I'm—I'm *afraid*!"

" My good man," said the lawyer, " try to make yourself clear. What are you afraid of?"

Poole seemed not to hear the question.

" I've been afraid for more than a week, sir," he said, " and I can't stand it any more."

The man's face bore out the truth of these words. He looked a frightened man, and, except for the moment when he had first spoken of his terror, he had not once looked the lawyer in the eyes. Even now, he was sitting there with the glass of wine untasted on his knee, and his eyes on a corner of the room. " I can't stand it any more," he repeated.

" Come," said the lawyer, in a sharp voice, " I've no doubt you have some reason for these words, Poole. Try to tell me what it is."

" I think there's been foul play," said Poole, hoarsely.

The lawyer stared at him.

" Foul play!" he cried. " What on earth do you mean?"

" I daren't say, sir," was the answer, " but will you come with me and see for yourself?"

Mr. Utterson did not hesitate. He rose and found his hat and coat. He saw, with wonder, the look of relief that at once showed itself upon Poole's face, and noticed that the wine was still untasted when he set down the glass.

It was a wild, cold night, with a pale moon and thin clouds flying across the sky. The wind made talking difficult, and seemed to have swept the streets bare of people. Mr. Utterson thought that never before had he seen that part of London so empty of passers-by.

The square, when they got there, was full of wind and dust, and the thin trees in the garden were bent over towards the ground. Poole stopped in the middle of the path. In spite of the biting weather, he took off his hat and wiped his face with a red handkerchief. His face was white and strained.

" Well, sir," he said, " we're here—and God grant there be nothing wrong."

He climbed the steps then, and knocked at the door in a guarded manner. Almost at once it was opened on the chain.

" Is that you, Poole?" asked a frightened voice within.

" It's all right," said Poole. " Open the door."

The hall, when they entered it, was brightly lit. The fire was built high, and all the servants stood close around it, like a flock of frightened sheep. At sight of Mr. Utterson, the house-maid burst into tears—of joy, no doubt; and the cook, crying out, " Bless God! it's Mr. Utterson," ran forward as if to take him in her arms.

" What are you all doing here?" asked the lawyer, angrily. " It will not please your master, you know."

" They're all afraid," said Poole.

A silence followed these words. No one denied their fright. Only the maid lifted up her voice, weeping all the more.

" Hold your tongue!" Poole said to her, and turned towards the boy who cleaned the knives.

" You," he ordered, " hand me a candle, and we'll see if we can get something done. Right! Now, Mr. Utterson, sir, will you please to follow me."

He led the way into the yard at the back.

" Now, sir," he said, in a voice that shook, " will you come as quietly as you can. I want you to hear, and I don't want you to be heard. And, sir—if by any chance the master asks you in, don't go."

At these last words, Mr. Utterson's nerves gave a big jump. But he took courage, and followed Poole to the foot of the stair that led up to the laboratory building. Here Poole signed to him to stand on one side and listen. He then climbed the steps, and knocked on the door.

" Mr. Utterson, sir, asking to see you," he called, and, as he did so, signed to the lawyer to listen very carefully.

" Tell him I cannot see anyone," answered a voice from within.

Mr. Utterson started. The voice was not Jekyll's, he was sure, and yet it was a voice that he had heard before. Whose?

" Thank you, sir," replied Poole, and he led the lawyer back across the yard and into the kitchen. There, he turned and stared straight into the lawyer's eyes.

" Well, sir," he said, " was that my master's voice?"

Mr. Utterson was pale and thoughtful.

" If it was," he said, " it has changed a great deal."

" Sir," said Poole, " I've been twenty years in this man's house, and I *know* it was not his voice. No, sir—my master's been *murdered*— he was murdered eight days ago, when we heard him cry out upon the name of God. But *who's* in there instead of him, and *why* does he stay there, Mr. Utterson?"

A terrible suspicion had entered the lawyer's mind. He thought he knew to whom that voice belonged. But he still could not believe that what Poole said was true.

" Supposing Dr. Jekyll *had* been murdered,"

he said, " why should the murderer stay here? It isn't sensible, Poole."

" Mr. Utterson, you are a hard man to satisfy," said Poole breathing hard, " but I'll do it yet. All this week, he, or it, or whatever is living in the laboratory, has been crying night and day for some sort of medicine that is badly needed. It has always been the master's habit to write his orders on a sheet of paper and leave it on the stair. We've had nothing else for more than a week past; nothing but papers, and a closed door; and even his food has been left on the stairs and taken in when nobody was looking. Well, sir, three or four times a day there have been orders and complaints, and I've been sent to every chemist in town. Every time I brought back the stuff he wanted, he'd put out another paper, after a time, telling me to return it because it wasn't pure, and to try again somewhere else. This drug is wanted badly, sir, whatever for."

" Have you any of these papers?" asked Mr. Utterson.

Poole felt in his pocket and handed over a paper which the lawyer read carefully. It was addressed to a wholesale chemist, and stated that the last quantity of a drug they had supplied was not pure and quite useless for Dr. Jekyll's purpose. In the year 1881, he had bought from

them a large quantity of the drug, and he begged
them to search and, should any of the same
quality be left, to forward it to him at once.

" For God's sake," he had added, at the
foot of the note, " find me some of the old."

" This is a strange note," said Mr. Utterson.
And then sharply, " How do you come to have
it open?"

" The man at the chemist's place was angry,
sir, and he threw it back at me," answered
Poole.

" There is no doubt that this is written in
the doctor's hand," went on the lawyer.

" I thought it looked like it, sir," replied
Poole. " But what does the writing matter?
I've seen him!"

" Seen him? Who?"

Poole's eyes opened wide with fear.

" Sir, I don't know," he whispered. " It
was this way. I came suddenly into the laboratory from the yard. He'd forgotten to lock
the door, sir. There he was at the far end of
the room, with a mask over his face, working
with his bottles and things. He looked up
when I came in, gave a kind of cry, and ran
into his study, at the other end of the laboratory.
It was only a second or two that I saw him, sir,
but the hair stood up straight on my head. If
that was my master, sir, why did he cry out

like a rat and run from me? And then . . ."

The man paused, and passed a hand over his face.

" Poole," said Mr. Utterson suddenly, " I think I see daylight. Perhaps your master is suffering from some disease that has altered his looks—there are such diseases—and needs this drug as a cure."

Poole shook his head and if anything, turned more pale than he was already.

" Sir," he said, " that thing I saw was not my master. I know it!" His voice sank to a whisper. " My master was a tall man, sir—the thing I saw was like a dwarf. No, sir, that thing in the mask was never Dr. Jekyll—God knows what it was, but it was *not* my master. I am sure that murder has been done——"

Mr. Utterson had made a decision.

" Poole," he said, and his face was very serious, " if you say that, then I consider it my duty to break in that door!"

" Ah, sir, now you're talking!" cried Poole. " There's an axe here, sir—and you might take the kitchen poker for yourself."

" One moment," said Mr. Utterson raising a hand. " It may be that you and I are about to place ourselves in a position of some danger. Tell me—did you recognize this masked figure that you saw?"

Poole looked him straight in the eye.

"If you mean, was it Mr. Hyde?—why, yes, I think it was! Who else could have got in by the laboratory door? You have not forgotten, sir, that at the time of the murder he still had the key with him? But that's not all. Did you ever meet this man Hyde, Mr. Utterson?"

"Yes," said the lawyer, "I once spoke with him."

"Then you must know that there was something queer about the gentleman—something that made you feel kind of cold inside."

"I know what you mean," said the lawyer quietly.

"Well, when that masked thing jumped like a monkey from among the chemicals, I felt that same feeling right down my back. I'm sure it was Mr. Hyde!"

"I think you may be right," returned the lawyer. "I believe poor Harry has been killed, and I believe that his murderer—for what reason, God alone can tell—is still in his victim's room. Well, we shall find out. Call Bradshaw."

The footman came quickly, looking very white and nervous.

"Bradshaw," said Mr. Utterson, "Poole and I are going to force our way into the laboratory. I want you and the boy to take two strong sticks and go round the corner by the outside door, in case anyone tries to make their escape that way. We will give you ten minutes to get to your stations.''

As Bradshaw left, the lawyer looked at his watch.

'' And now, Poole,'' he said, '' let us stand ready by the door.''

He took up the kitchen poker, Poole lifted a large axe, and they went into the yard. The clouds had closed over the moon, and it was now quite dark. When they came to the foot of the laboratory steps, they sat down silently to wait. London hummed solemnly all around; but nearer at hand the stillness was only broken by the sound of a footfall moving to and fro beyond the door.

'' So it will walk all day, sir,'' whispered Poole, '' and most of the night, too. Listen carefully, sir, and tell me—is that the doctor's step?''

The steps fell lightly and oddly. They were very different indeed from the heavy tread of Henry Jekyll. Mr. Utterson shook his head sadly, then the pair just sat and listened to the steps going up and down . . .

The ten minutes drew to an end. Mr. Utterson lifted a finger, Poole rose and set the candle upon a higher stair. They hesitated a moment longer, listening to that patient footfall still going up and down in the quiet night.

"Jekyll," cried Utterson, in a loud voice, "I demand to see you." He paused, but there was no reply. "I must warn you that we are about to break in the door!"

"Utterson," cried a voice, "for God's sake, have mercy!"

"That's not Jekyll's voice—it's Hyde's!" cried the lawyer. "Down with the door, Poole!"

Poole swung the axe over his shoulder. The blow shook the building and the door seemed to jump against the lock. Inside, there was a dismal scream, as of an animal in terror. Four times the axe fell, but the wood was tough, and it was not until the fifth stroke that the lock broke away and the wreck of the door fell in upon the carpet.

In the sudden quiet, the two stood still, their hearts beating fast and loud, and stared into the laboratory. Nothing moved in there. Mr. Utterson took a deep breath and stepped into the room, moved forward, and came to a dead stop, a little cry breaking from his lips.

Right in the middle of the room, there lay the body of a man, his face to the floor. Mr. Utterson signed for Poole to follow him. They drew near, turned it on its back, and saw the face of Edward Hyde.

CHAPTER ELEVEN

The Disappearance

ONE glance at that face told Utterson that Hyde was dead. He was astonished to see that the man was dressed in clothes that were far too big for him; and, by the blue glass bottle that the man held in his hand, and the sharp smell that hung still upon the air, he knew that he was looking on the body of a self-destroyer.

" We have come too late," he said slowly, " either to save or punish. It only remains for us to find the body of your master."

The greater part of the building was occupied by the laboratory, and by the study, which formed a separate room at one end and looked down upon the court. A passage joined the laboratory to the door on the side street. There were, besides, a few large cupboards and a cellar. All these they now searched. Nowhere was there a trace of Henry Jekyll, dead or alive.

Poole stamped a foot down hard on the stones of the passage.

" He must be buried here," he said,
" though I see no signs of the stones having
been lifted."

" Or he may have gone out that way," said
Utterson, and turned to examine the door into
the side street. It was locked, and lying near
by upon the ground they found the key,
broken and stained with rust.

" It looks as if a man has stamped on it,"
said Poole.

The lawyer raised a hand to his head.

" This is beyond me, Poole," he said. " Let
us go back to the laboratory."

They entered the laboratory once more and,
with an occasional glance at the dead body,
began to look more carefully about the place.
At one table there were traces of chemical
work; various measured heaps of some white
salt, made it look as though the man had been
interrupted in the middle of an experiment.

" Sir, that's the same drug that I was always
bringing him," said Poole, pointing, and then
his glance went to the long mirror that Utterson had noticed before.

" That glass has seen some strange things,
sir," whispered Poole.

" And none stranger than itself," echoed
the lawyer. " What on earth could Jekyll
have wanted with it?"

He put the glass to his lips and drank. (Page 82)

" I don't know, sir," answered Poole, " but I've often wondered."

Next they turned to the business table. On it lay a large envelope, and Utterson gave a start when he saw his own name written upon it in the doctor's hand. He opened it, and some papers fell to the floor. The first was a will, drawn up in the same strange terms as the one he had returned six months before, to serve in case of *the disappearance* of Henry Jekyll; but in place of the name of Edward Hyde, the lawyer, in great astonishment, read his own. He looked at Poole, and then back at the papers, and last of all at the dead man stretched out upon the carpet.

" My head is going round," he said. " That man has been shut in here for days, and he has not destroyed this will."

He looked at the next paper. It was a brief note in the doctor's hand and dated at the top.

" Poole!" he cried. " He was alive and here this day. But where has he gone? Can we be sure that Hyde took his own life? We must be careful, or we may yet drag your master into some serious trouble."

" Sir, why don't you read what he says?" asked Poole, looking very worried.

Utterson looked at the paper, and read as follows:

My dear Utterson,

When this falls into your hands, I shall have disappeared. There is no other way for it. Go then, and first read the narrative which Lanyon warned me he was about to place in your hands; and if you care to hear more, turn to the confession of—

> Your unworthy and unhappy friend,
>
> Henry Jekyll.

" There was this, too, sir," said Poole, and handed Utterson a second envelope sealed in several places.

The lawyer put it in his pocket. ' I would say nothing of this to anyone," he said seriously. " If your master has run away, or is dead, we may at least save his good name. It is now ten o'clock. I must go home and read these documents in quiet—but I shall be back before midnight, when we shall send for the police."

They went out, and locked the door of the laboratory behind them. Utterson left the servants gathered once more about the fire in the hall, and walked back to his office to read the two narratives in which the mystery was to be explained.

CHAPTER TWELVE

Dr. Lanyon's Statement

ON the 9th of January, now four days ago, I had by the evening post a registered envelope addressed to me in the hand of my old school friend, Henry Jekyll. I was surprised by this, for I had dined with the man the night before, and I could imagine nothing that might have happened to make him take this step. The contents increased my wonder; for this is how the letter ran:

Dear Lanyon,

You are one of my oldest friends, and, though we may not always have seen eye to eye on scientific questions, I do not think there has been any real break in our friendship. Lanyon, my life is at your mercy. If you fail me tonight I am lost.

I ask you, no matter what other affairs you may have on hand, to drive straight to my house when you have read these words. Poole has his orders; you will find him waiting your arrival with a locksmith. The door of my study is then to be forced. You are to go in alone, open the cupboard door on the left hand, breaking the lock if it be shut, and to take out the fourth drawer from the top. You may know the right drawer by its contents: some powders, a bottle, and a paper book. This drawer I beg of you to carry to Cavendish Square.

You should be back before midnight. At that time, I ask you to be alone in your consulting-room, and to admit into the house by your own hand a man who will present himself in my name, and to give him the drawer that you will have brought from the study. Then you will have played your part and earned my gratitude completely. Five minutes afterwards, if you insist upon an explanation, you will see that these arrangements are of the first import-ance to me. If you fail me, indeed, I am sure that you will have my death on your conscience.

My hand trembles at the bare thought of such a possibility. Think of me at this hour, in a strange place and in a dark despair, and know that if you serve me as I ask, my troubles will roll away like a story that is told. Serve me, my dear Lanyon, and save

Your friend,

H. J.

When I had read this letter, I felt sure that

my friend was mad—but until I knew that for certain I felt bound to do as he asked. I rose at once and drove straight to Jekyll's house. Poole was awaiting my arrival, and a locksmith with him. We moved at once to Jekyll's study. The door was very strong, and it took the locksmith almost an hour to open it. The cupboard that Jekyll had mentioned was not locked, and I took out the drawer, tied it in a sheet, and returned with it to Cavendish Square.

Here I examined its contents. The powders, I thought, were of Jekyll's own manufacture. The bottle was about half full of a blood-red liquid. The book contained little but a series of dates, made over many years, ending suddenly nearly a year ago. All this stirred my curiosity, but told me nothing. How these things could mean life or death to Jekyll I could not make out. The more I thought about it, indeed, the more sure I became that I was dealing with a madman—and, though I sent my servants off to bed, I loaded an old revolver, that I might have some weapon to defend myself if the need arose.

Twelve o'clock had scarce rung out over London, when the knocker sounded very gently on the door. I went myself, and found a small man waiting on the step.

" Are you from Dr. Jekyll?" I asked.

He nodded quickly, and I told him to enter. He first gave a searching backward glance into the darkness of the square. There was a policeman not far off, advancing with a lantern; and at the sight I thought my visitor started and made greater haste. I did not at all like the look of this, and as I followed him into the bright light of the consulting-room I kept my hand ready on my revolver.

I sat down and studied him closely. He was small, as I have said; I was struck by the shocking expression of his face; and, also, by a strong feeling of dislike, or disgust, that I felt to an almost sickening extent.

He was dressed in the most odd way. His clothes, though of good cloth, were enormously too large for him—the trousers hanging on his legs and rolled up to keep them from the ground, the bottom of the jacket almost to his knees, and the collar opening wide upon his shoulders. Strange to say I had no wish to laugh at him, but rather felt a kind of fear.

My visitor was on fire with excitement.

" Have you got it?" he cried. " Have you got it?" As he spoke he laid his hand upon my arm.

I pushed him back, for at his touch I felt a coldness run through my blood, and a new feeling of horror touched me to the heart. I was still very curious, however, and I wanted to see what would happen next.

"There it is, sir," I said, pointing to the drawer, as it lay on the floor behind a table, still covered with the sheet.

He sprang to it, and then paused, and laid his hand upon his heart. He showed me his teeth in a terrible smile that was like the snarl of a dog, and his face was twisted as though it were made of rubber. He looked so awful, standing there, that I grew alarmed for his life and reason.

"Steady yourself," I said.

As if with the decision of despair, he tore off the sheet. At sight of the contents, he gave a cry of such immense relief as I had never heard before. And the next moment, in a voice that was already fairly well under control, "Have you a measuring-glass?" he asked.

I gave him what he wanted. He thanked me with a smiling nod, measured out a few drops of the red liquid and added one of the powders. The liquid began to brighten in colour, and to throw off small fumes of vapour. Suddenly the mixture changed to a deep purple, which faded again more slowly to a watery green. My visitor smiled as if well satisfied, set down the glass upon the table, and then turned and looked at me with narrowed eyes.

" And now," he said, " will you allow me
to take this glass in my hand and leave your
house without further question? Or is your
curiosity too much for you? No, think before
you answer. If I go now, you will be left as
you were before, neither richer nor wiser. If
you prefer otherwise, a new field of knowledge
shall be opened to you, here, in this room, on
the instant. You will see something, sir, that
will astonish you, believe me!"

There was something in his manner—a kind
of threat—that I did not like at all. I looked
at him calmly enough, however, and answered:
" Your words make little sense to me, but I
have gone too far in this thing to stop before I
see the end."

" Very well," replied my visitor, with his
twisted smile. " Lanyon, you remember your
vows? What follows is under the seal of our
profession. And now you—who sneered at my
experiments, and treated your betters with
scorn—see!"

He put the glass to his lips, and drank, with
one swift movement. A cry followed; he almost
fell, but seized hold of the table, staring with
fixed eyes and open mouth; and as I looked,
there came a change—he seemed to swell—
his face became suddenly black, and the features
seemed to melt and alter . . . The next

moment I had sprung to my feet and backed against the wall, my arm raised to shield me from that—that monster, my mind filled with terror.

There before my eyes—pale and shaken, and half fainting, and feeling before him with his hands, like a man restored from death—*there stood Henry Jekyll!*

What he told me in the next hour I cannot bring my mind to set on paper. I saw what I saw, I heard what I heard, and my soul sickened at it. My life is shaken to its roots; sleep has left me; a deadly terror sits by me at all hours of the day and night. I feel that my days are numbered, and that I must die; and yet I shall die refusing to believe what has so shaken me and that I saw with my own eyes. As for the evil and wicked things that man showed me, I cannot, even in memory, think of it without a start of horror. I will say one last thing, Utterson and that—if you can bring your mind to believe it—will be more than enough . . .

The creature who crept into my house that night was, on Jekyll's own confession, known by the name of Hyde and hunted for in every corner of the land as the murderer of Carew.

Hastie Lanyon.

CHAPTER THIRTEEN

Henry Jekyll's Full Statement of the Case

I WAS born in 1825 to a large fortune; and, at a fairly early age, discovered that I had a taste for science, and was intelligent enough, and rich enough, to follow any line of scientific inquiry which appealed to me. I was fond of the respect of my fellow men, and it seemed certain that a distinguished future lay before me.

My chief fault was the fact that I had a liking for gaiety, and there was a certain wildness in my nature which did not fit in with the common picture of a grave and learned doctor or scientist. I found it hard to combine these tastes with the image I wished to present before the public eye. So it came about that I took my pleasures—and was guilty of many sins—in secret, behind locked doors, and without beat of drum.

When I reached years of reflection, and began to look round me and take stock of my progress and position in the world, I saw that I had, in fact lived not one life—but two. Most men would have cared nothing for the sins I had committed, but the better side of my nature regarded them, and hid them, with a strong sense of shame. It seemed to me that, although all men are made up of good and evil parts, in my own case the dividing line was most clearly marked. At various times, and according to the mood of the hour, I was either completely bad, or wished to do only what was good and right.

Whichever side of me was in control, however, I was always in earnest. I was as much myself when I performed an evil deed, in the dark of night, as when I worked, in the eye of day, at the relief of pain and suffering.

It chanced that my scientific studies, which led towards the mystic, began to throw a strong light on this consciousness of the two sides of my nature. With every day that passed, I drew steadily nearer to the truth by the discovery of which I have been brought to ruin and disgrace: that man is not truly one, but truly two. I say two, because that state of my knowledge does not pass beyond that point. Others will follow and develop my work farther than I have dreamed. For my part, I advanced in one direction only. It was on the moral side,

and in my own person, that I learned to recognize the two sides of my nature; I saw that,
even if I could rightly be said to be either, it
was only because I was *both*. I began to consider the possibilty of separating these two
elements. Was it possible, I asked myself, that
each could be set free to go its own way? Was
it not the curse of mankind that these two
elements were thus bound together, and always
struggling to gain the upper hand? But how
could they be separated?

I was so far in my reflections when a light
started to shine upon the subject from the
laboratory table. My experiments began to
reveal to me how airy and shadowy was this
so-called solid body in which we walk. Certain
chemical agents I found to have the power to
change and shake off the screen of flesh behind
which we live. I will not enter deeply into this
scientific part of my confession. First, because
I have been made to learn that the weighty cares
of our life are bound for ever on man's shoulders;
and, when the attempt is made to throw them
aside, they return upon us with more awful
pressure. Second, because, as this narrative
will make only too clear, my discoveries were
not complete. Enough, then, that I managed
to produce a drug by which the evil powers
within me took complete control of my mind

and had so marked an effect upon my body, because they were still the expression of a natural part of me, that my features and outward form became changed beyond recognition.

I hesitated a long time before I put this drug to the test of practice. I knew that I risked death in taking it, for any drug that controlled and shook my being to such an extent might destroy the feeble body that I looked to it to change. My eagerness to test so strange a discovery, however, at last persuaded me to make the experiment. I had long since prepared what I had best call, simply, the *liquid* that I needed; I obtained at once from a firm of wholesale chemists, a large quantity of a particular salt, which I knew from my experiments to be the element most required. Then, late one night, I mixed my drug, watched it boil and smoke in the glass, and, with a strong glow of courage, I drank.

I suffered the most terrible pains, as if my bones were being broken on the wheel, a deadly sickness, and a horror of the spirit that cannot be exceeded at the hour of birth or death. Then, as the sickness and the pain began to die away, I came to myself as if after a long illness. There was something strange in my sensations, something new and wonderfully pleasant. I felt younger, lighter, happier in body; the blood

seemed to race quicker through my veins; I
was conscious of a new, devil-may-care feeling
that burned in me like a flame. I knew myself,
at the first breath of this new life, to be far
more wicked, and quite full of original evil. In
that moment, the thought delighted me like
wine. I stretched out my hands, enjoying the
wonderful freshness of these sensations—and
was suddenly aware that I had become much
smaller than the big strong, Dr. Jekyll whom
all the world knew.

There was no mirror, at that date, in my
room. The one that you have seen was brought
there later on. The night, however, was far
gone into the morning; my servants were all
fast asleep; and I decided to walk in my new
shape as far as my bedroom. I crossed the
yard, where the stars must have looked down
upon me with wonder, as a kind of creature
that even they had never seen before. I crept
through the silent passages, a stranger in my
own house, and, when I came to my own
room, I saw for the first time the appearance
of Edward Hyde.

It was clear to me at once that the evil side
of my nature was less developed than the good,
which, for the moment, it had driven out.
Again, in the course of my life, which had been
largely a life of effort, goodness and control,

the evil had been much less exercised, and so had all the more vigour now. It was because of this, I think, that Edward Hyde was so much smaller and younger than Henry Jekyll. While good shone upon the face of the one, evil was written plainly on the face of the other. Evil, besides, had left upon Hyde's body a suggestion of deformity and decay. Yet, when I looked upon that ugly image before me, I felt no disgust, but rather a feeling of welcome. It was, in my eyes, a true image of the spirit; it seemed far more real than the divided character I had called my own.

So far, no doubt, I was right. I have noticed, when I wore the shape of Edward Hyde, that none could come near to me without a feeling of horror. This, as I saw it, was because all human beings are made up of good and evil: but Edward Hyde, alone in the ranks of mankind, was pure evil.

I stayed only a moment or two before the mirror. A second experiment had yet to be made. It remained to be seen if I could call back the shape of Dr. Henry Jekyll, or whether I must creep, like a thief in the night, from a house that was no longer mine. Hurrying back to my laboratory, I once more prepared and drank the cup, once more suffered the same pains, and came to myself once more with the

character, the larger build and the face of
Henry Jekyll.

That night I had come to the crossroads. If
I had approached my discovery in a more noble
spirit, all might yet have been well. The drug
had no ill-effects, but it had shaken the prison-
house of my nature, and that which had been
shut up within had now been given the chance
to go free. The evil within me was quick to
seize its chance.

Even at that time, I had not yet conquered
the wildness in my nature and my liking for
pleasure, as a relief from the dryness of study.
As I was not only well known and highly
considered, but growing towards an old man,
this side of my life held certain dangers for me.
It was on this side that my new power tempted
me. I had but to drink the cup to throw off the
body of the famous doctor, and put on, like a
change of clothing, the shape of Edward Hyde.
I smiled at the idea. It seemed, at that time,
amusing; and I made my preparations with
great care.

I took, and furnished, that house in Soho to
which Hyde was tracked by the police. I
engaged as housekeeper a creature whom I
well knew to be silent and wicked at heart. In
my own home, I announced to my servants that
a Mr. Hyde, whom I described to them, was to

have full liberty and power about my house in the square, and was to be obeyed in all things as I was myself. I even called, and made myself a familiar object in my second character. Next, I drew up that will to which you so strongly objected; then, if anything happened to me in the person of Dr. Jekyll, I could enter on that of Edward Hyde without the loss of my riches. And so, having made myself safe from attack— as I thought—I began to take advantage of the powers given to me by my discovery.

Men have often hired others to carry out their crimes, while their own person and reputation sat under shelter. I was the first that ever did so for my own pleasure. I was the first that could walk in the public eye and be respected by all—and then, in a moment, throw off the old, familiar shape and put on a new. And, for me, the safety was complete. Think of it— I did not even exist! Let me but escape into my laboratory, give me but a second or two to swallow the drug that I had always standing ready, and, whatever he had done, Edward Hyde would pass away like the stain of breath upon a mirror. In his place, working quietly at home, would be Henry Jekyll—a man who could afford to laugh at suspicion.

I made a number of excursions, usually at night, in the character of Edward Hyde, in search of pleasures that were denied to the honest doctor. When I returned, I was often filled with a kind of wonder at the wickedness of which I had found myself capable. The being that I had called out of my own soul, and sent out alone to take his pleasure, was a creature of evil and as hard as stone. His every act and thought centred on self. At times, Henry Jekyll looked back in horror at the deeds of Edward Hyde; but the situation was apart from ordinary laws, and it was Hyde alone that was guilty. Jekyll was no worse for it; he woke again to his own good qualities and would even make haste, where it was possible, to undo the evil worked by Hyde. And so time passed and Jekyll's conscience slept quietly . . .

I will not tell you of all the sins committed by Edward Hyde. I mean but to point out the warnings and the steps which have led me to my punishment and my end. I met with one accident which, as it brought no serious consequence, I shall no more than mention. An act of cruelty to a child stirred the anger of a passer-by, whom I saw the other day in your company; the doctor and the child's family joined him against me; there were moments, even, when I feared for my life. At last, in order to calm them all down, Edward Hyde had to bring them to the door, and pay them with a

cheque drawn in the name of Henry Jekyll.
This danger, in the future, was easily ruled out
by opening an account at another bank in the
name of Edward Hyde himself; and when, by
sloping my own hand backwards, I had supplied
my double with a signature, I thought I sat
beyond the reach of fate.

Some two months before the murder of Sir
Danvers, I had been out for one of my adventures, had returned at a late hour, and woke
the next day in bed with odd sensations. It
was in vain I looked about me; in vain I saw
the familiar furniture of my own room in the
square; something still kept telling me that I
was not where I was, that I had not wakened
where I seemed to be, but in the little room in
Soho where I was accustomed to sleep in the
body of Edward Hyde. I smiled, and asked
myself what could cause this feeling. And then
my eye fell upon my hand . . .

Now, the hand of Henry Jekyll—as you have
often seen—was large and firm, white and
shapely. But the hand which I now saw clearly
enough, in the yellow light of a mid-London
morning, lying there on the bed-clothes, was
lean, knotted, brown, and covered with a thick
growth of dark hair. It was the hand of Edward
Hyde.

I was astonished. I must have stared at it

for nearly a minute, simply lost in wonder, before terror awoke inside me as sudden as the crash of a gun. I jumped from my bed; rushed to my mirror. At the sight that met my eyes, my blood was changed into something thin and icy. I had gone to bed Henry Jekyll, I had awakened Edward Hyde! How was this to be explained, I asked myself. And, with another great start of terror, how was it to be remedied? It was well on in the morning; the servants were up; all my drugs were in the laboratory —a long journey, down two flights of stairs, through the back passage, and across the yard. It might indeed be possible to cover my face, but what use was that when I could not hide the change in size? And then, with a strong sense of relief, I realized that the servants were already used to the coming and going of my second self. I dressed, as well as I was able, in clothes of Edward Hyde's size. I passed through the house, where Bradshaw stared and drew back at seeing Mr. Hyde at such an hour and in such odd clothing; and ten minutes later Dr. Jekyll had returned to his own shape, and was sitting down, pretending to have an appetite for his breakfast.

This strange happening frightened me, I must confess. I began to reflect more seriously than ever before on the issues and possibilities of my double existence. That hidden part of me which I now had the power to call into existence had been much exercised in the past few months. It now seemed to me as though the body of Edward Hyde had grown stronger and taller and I began to see a danger. If I gave him too much liberty, the balance of my nature might be quite overthrown, and the character of Edward Hyde become mine for the rest of my days. The drug had not always worked successfully. Once, very early in my experiments, it had failed me altogether. Since then I had been obliged on more than one occasion to double the amount, and several times, at risk of death, to take three times the quantity I had first thought necessary.

Now, however, and in the light of the morning's accident, I saw that where, in the beginning, the difficulty had been to throw off the body of Jekyll, it had of late been the other way about. All things therefore seemed to point to this: that I was beginning to lose hold of my original and better self, and becoming slowly more and more absorbed with my second and worse.

Between these two I now felt I had to choose. My two natures had memory in common, but little else was equally shared between them. Jekyll, who was a combination of both, was

sometimes frightened by Hyde, but could also
share in his pleasures and adventures; but
Hyde cared nothing for Jekyll. Jekyll had more
than a father's interest; Hyde had more than
a son's unconcern.

To stamp out Hyde and to remain only
Jekyll, was to lose for ever those pleasures
which I had so much enjoyed. To surrender to
Hyde was to lose all touch with my work and
interests, and to become, in an instant, friend-
less and alone in the world. Strange as my
circumstances were, the terms of this debate
are as old as man himself; and it fell out with
me, as it falls with most men, that I chose the
better part, and was found wanting in the
strength to keep to it.

Yes, I preferred the ageing and discontented
doctor, surrounded by friends, and filled with
honest hopes; and I said a determined farewell
to the liberty, the comparative youth, the
light step, the racing blood and secret pleasures
of Edward Hyde. Perhaps I was not honest
with myself, for I neither gave up the house in
Soho, nor destroyed the clothes of Edward
Hyde, which still lay ready in my study. For
two months, however, I was true to my deter-
mination; for two months I led a life of
wonderful goodness. But then I began to feel
longings, as of Hyde struggling after freedom,

and at last, in an hour of weakness, I once again mixed and swallowed the drug.

Even then, I suppose, I had not made enough allowance for the terrible readiness to evil which were the leading characteristics of Edward Hyde. Yet it was by these that I was punished. My devil had been kept too long in his cage. He came out roaring. I was conscious, even when I took the drug, of a stronger leaning towards evil . . .

It must have been this that brought Edward Hyde to murder. I remember how impatiently I listened to the polite words of that poor old man, who was my victim. I declare before God that no man in his moral senses could have been guilty of so terrible a crime without cause or reason; and that I struck him down in the same spirit in which a sick child may break a toy.

The spirit of evil awoke in me that night and was beyond all control. I hit that helpless old man, and rained blow after blow upon him, tasting delight in my own cruelty. It was not till I grew weary that I was suddenly struck through the heart by a cold thrill of terror. I saw that what I had done could cost me my life and I ran to the house in Soho, with no pity inside me, but trembling for my own safety. I destroyed my papers, and then set out through the lamplit streets, still glorying in my crime—even planning others for the future— and yet still listening behind me for the steps that might mean I was discovered. Hyde had a song on his lips as he mixed the drug, but the pains that followed had not done tearing him before Henry Jekyll, weeping tears of pity, had fallen upon his knees and lifted his hands to God.

In that hour I saw my life as a whole. I followed it up from the days of childhood, when I had walked with my father's hand, and through the years of my professional life, to arrive again and again at the unbelievable horrors of that night. I could have screamed aloud. I tried with tears and prayers to hold back the crowd of ugly images with which my mind was filled. And then a new thought came to me. The problem of my conduct was solved. From that moment on, Hyde was impossible. I had no choice but to live in the character of Henry Jekyll, and to be guided by the better part of my existence. To make quite sure that evil was put behind me, I locked the door in the side street, by which I had so often gone and come, and broke the key under my heel!

The next day came the news that the murder had been seen by a girl sitting at a window, that all London knew that Hyde was guilty, and that the victim was a man held high in the public regard. It was not only a crime, it had been an act of madness. I think I was glad to know it; I was glad to have my better nature guarded by the terrors of the gallows that waited for Edward Hyde. Jekyll was now my only shelter; let Hyde peep out but for an instant, and the hands of all men would be raised to take and kill him.

I resolved, in my future conduct, to do what I could to repair the evil of the past. I can say with honesty that my resolve produced some good. You know yourself how earnestly in the last months of this past year I worked to relieve suffering; you know that much was done for others, and that the days passed quietly, almost happily, for myself. I can truly say that I did not weary of this good and innocent life; I think, instead, that I daily enjoyed it more completely; but I was still cursed by the lower side of me, so recently chained down, and as the time passed it began to demand its freedom. Not that I dreamed of giving life and form to Edward Hyde once more. The bare idea of that would fill me with horror. No, it was in my own person, as an ordinary secret sinner, that I at last gave way to temptation.

There comes an end to all things; and this surrender to my evil at last destroyed the balance of my soul. And yet I was not greatly worried; the fall seemed natural, like a return to the old days before I had made my discovery . . .

It was a fine, clear January day, and I sat in the sun on a bench in Regent's Park, feeling sleepy and at rest. After all, I remember thinking, I was like my neighbours; and then I smiled, comparing myself with other men, and thinking how much good I had done of late. And at the very moment the thought entered my head, a sickness came over me, with all the old pains, and that horror of the spirit that I knew so well. These passed away and left me faint. And then, as the faintness left me in its turn, I began to be aware of a change in the direction of my thoughts, a greater courage, a lack of care for danger. I looked down. My clothes hung loosely upon my limbs and the hand that lay on my knee was lean and hairy. I was once more Edward Hyde. A moment before I had been safe, respected, wealthy—the cloth being laid for me in the dining-room at home; and now I was hunted, houseless, a known murderer, with every man's hand against me.

My reason did not fail me, and Hyde rose to the importance of the moment. My drugs were locked away in a cupboard in my study; how was I to reach them? That was the problem I set myself to solve. The laboratory door I had closed. If I tried to enter by the house, my own servants would seize me, and call for the police. I saw that I must employ another hand, and thought of Lanyon. How was he to be reached, how persuaded? Supposing that I escaped capture in the streets, how was I to make my way into his presence? And how should I, an unknown and unwanted visitor, persuade the famous doctor to break into the study of his fellow-worker, Dr. Jekyll? Then I remembered that of my original character one part still remained to me: I could write my own hand. Once I remembered that, I saw the way that I must follow.

At once, I arranged my clothes as best I could, called a cab, and drove to an hotel in Portland Street, the name of which I chanced to remember. At my appearance, the driver burst into a laugh. I turned upon him with a look of devilish anger, and the smile vanished from his face—happily for him—yet more happily for myself, for in another instant I would have set hands on him and killed him. At the hotel, as I entered, I stared about me with so terrible a look that I saw the servants tremble. There was no laughter at my expense. They led me to a private room, and brought me pen and paper. Hyde in danger of his life was a creature new to me: shaken with anger,

ready to murder, longing to strike and inflict
pain.   Yet the creature mastered his temper
with a great effort of will; wrote two letters,
one to Lanyon and one to Poole, and sent them
out with directions that they should be registered.

For the rest of that day, he sat over the fire
in the private room, biting his nails, and trying
to control his anger.   There he dined, sitting
alone with his fears; and from there, when
night came, he set out in the corner of a closed
cab, and was driven to and fro about the streets
of the city.   He, I say—I cannot say, I.   That
child of the devil had nothing human about
him; nothing lived in him but fear and hatred.
And when at last, thinking the driver had
begun to grow suspicious, he paid off the cab
and went on foot, dressed in his odd clothing,
among the walkers of the night, his fear and
his anger raged like a storm within him.   He
walked fast, hunted by his fears, choosing the
darkest and quietest streets, counting the minutes that still divided him from midnight.
Once a woman spoke to him, offering a box of
lights.   He struck her in the face, and she ran
from him, crying.

When I came to myself at Lanyon's, the
horror of my old friend affected me perhaps: I
do not know; it was at least but a drop in the

sea to the horror with which Henry Jekyll looked back upon the past ten hours. I gave little thought to the words in which Lanyon cursed and condemned me. It was partly in a dream that I came home to my own house and got into bed. I slept well after the cares of the day and awoke weakened but refreshed. I still hated, and feared, the thought of the brute that slept within me, and I had not, of course, forgotten the awful dangers of the day before; but I was once more at home, in my own house and close to my drugs; and gratitude for my escape filled the whole of my being.

I was walking across the yard after breakfast, when I was seized again with the pains and sensations that went before the change of character. I only had time to gain the shelter of my laboratory, before I was once again experiencing the rage and hatreds of Edward Hyde. It took on this occasion a double dose to bring back Henry Jekyll; and, alas! six hours after, as I sat looking sadly into the fire, the pains returned, and the drug had to be taken once more. In short, from that day on it seemed only by a great effort, and only through the immediate swallowing of the drug, that I was able to wear the shape of Jekyll. At all hours of the day and night, I would be taken with the violent trembling that was the first warning of

a change of shape and character. Above all, if
I slept, or even nodded off for a moment in my
chair, it was always as Hyde that I awakened.
Under the strain of the sleeplessness to which
I now condemned myself, I became, in my own
person, a creature eaten up and emptied by
fever, weak both in mind and body, and occupied by only one thought: the horror of my
other self. And when I did sleep, or when the
effect of the drug wore off, I would spring
almost without thought now—for the pains
grew daily less marked—into the possession of
a fancy filled with images of terror, a soul
boiling with causeless hatreds, and a body that
seemed not strong enough to contain the life
that raged within. The powers of Hyde seemed
to have grown with the sickness of Jekyll. And
certainly, the hate that now divided them, was
equal on each side.

Jekyll had now seen to the full the evil of
the creature that shared with him the body of
one man; knew only too well the devil that
lay caged in his flesh, where he heard it mutter
and felt it struggle to be born. The hatred of
Hyde for Jekyll was of a different order. His
terror of the gallows drove him, for a time, to
return to the shelter of Jekyll's body; but he
hated the dislike that Jekyll had for him, and
indeed, had it not been for his fear of death, he

would long ago have ruined himself in order to bring me to ruin. But his love of life is wonderful; I go further; I, who sicken and freeze at the mere thought of him, still find it in my heart to pity him, when I remember how he fears my power to cut him off by suicide.

It is useless, and the time fails me, to drag out this description. No one, I think has ever suffered as I have these past few weeks. And my punishment might have gone on for years, but for the blow which now has fallen. My supply of essential salt began to run low. I sent out for a fresh supply and mixed the drug; the first change of colour followed, but not the second. I drank it, and it had no effect. You will have heard from Poole how I have searched London for the quality I need. It has all been in vain. I am now persuaded that my first supply was not pure, and it was that which gave the mixture its power.

About a week had passed, and I am now finishing this statement under the influence of the last of the old powders. This, then, is the last time that Henry Jekyll can think his own thoughts or see his own face in the glass. Nor must I delay too long to bring my writing to an end; for if my narrative has so far escaped destruction by Hyde, it has been by a combination of care and good luck. Should my shape

change while I am writing it, Hyde will tear it
in pieces; but if some time shall have passed
after I have laid it by, his wonderful selfishness
will probably save it once again from the action
of his ape-like spirit. And indeed the fate that
is closing on us both has already changed and
crushed him.

Half an hour from now, when I shall again
take on the shape of that hated creature of my
own making, I know how I shall sit weeping
and trembling in my chair, listening to every
sound outside, and fearing the punishment for
his crime . . .

Will Hyde die upon the gallows, or will he
find the courage to release himself, at the last
moment? God knows; I care not; this is my
true hour of death, and what is to follow con-
cerns another than myself. Here, then, as I lay
down the pen, and seal up my confession, I
bring the life of that unhappy Henry Jekyll to
an end.

Blackie & Son, Ltd.,
©
1962